The Pocket Guide to Gobline

Written and Illustrated by Jessica Cathryn Feinberg

With special thanks to:

All fans, friends and Kickstarter backers whose support made this book possible.

To Tony for inspiration & very bad jokes!

My editor - Victoria Morris
My proofreaders - Gemma & Michelle

FIRST EDITION MAY 2015

ISBN: 978-1-943275-20-5

WHAT ARE GOBLINS?

Early records of goblins date back as far as the 14th century. Over time the word "Goblin" has had various spellings including gobblin, gobeline, goblyn, gobling, and gobbeline.

The term usually refers to a type of Fae creature with extremely long, pointed ears and a mischievous nature.

Goblins can be found all over the world and come in many different sizes and sub-species including Hobgoblins, Kobolds, Trow, and Knockers.

This guide will help you identify different types of goblins and teach you about their culture - including diet, socialization, inventing, sports and so forth.

WARNING: Most goblins are not evil, but almost all have a insatiable mischievous nature so they should always be approached with care. Never try to trap, imprison, or harm a goblin. This can bring about a vicious backlash of goblin pranks - sometimes even deadly ones.

Should you encounter a troublesome goblin or have a goblin infestation please see the information on dealing with goblin problems that is included at the end of this book.

Common Goblins

All goblins have long, pointed ears. Many also have long noses and are skinny with spindly limbs. A few goblins have been known to be more rotund. This is usually job related (i.e. goblin cooks are often heavier). Some goblins also have tails, but it is rare. The most common type of goblin found in homes and gardens is fairly small - generally under a foot high - which helps them go unnoticed.

Knockers

The Knocker or Knacker is most often found in Wales, Cornwall, and Devon.

They are two to three feet in height and usually very dirty from spending their days in mine shafts and tunnels.

The name "Knocker" comes from the sounds this goblin makes in mines. It is said if you hear them knocking, a cave-in is soon to follow. It has never been clear if the goblins are the cause of the cave-in, or if they are simply warning others of the danger.

Kobolds

The German Kobold is one of the largest goblins, sometimes mistaken for a small child at a distance. Often Kobolds are linked to a specific household and will either help or hinder the residents depending on how the home is treated. A Kobold might help with chores one day and hide your glasses the next. These goblins are very quiet and fast moving which often causes them to be mistaken for spirits or ghosts.

A trail of sawdust or wood chips near the front door is usually the sign of a Kobold moving in.

Hobgoblins

Hobgoblins are a cross breed of House Brownies and Goblins. They are a bit larger than the Common Goblin, with a much more stocky build and tend to be a lot more hairy.

While they may still be helpful around the house or garden, Hobgoblins are much more mischievous than Brownies. They are pranksters by nature, though their pranks are more inconvenient than harmful. Milk spoiling for no reason and mysteriously flat tires are signs you may have a Hobgoblin around.

When they rarely speak to humans these creatures speak in taunting rhymes and often leap about while reciting them. When happy they can be very helpful and protective of the household and are generally more likely to play pranks on visitors than those who live in the home (they enjoy the embarrassment of the residents).

While these are similar creatures to Boggarts (abused house Brownies), it should be noted that Boggarts tend to be more vicious with their anger and are not, in fact, a type of goblin species.

Hobgoblins are often distressed if the home is neglected. To pacify an upset Hobgoblin leave it small, but expensive gifts and make home improvements.

Trow

The Scottish Trow is a mix of troll, goblin and fairy that primarily dwells in the Orkney and Shetland Islands. These creatures are much smaller and shorter than humans, but larger than most other goblins.

Trow make their dens in knowes (ancient mounds of earth) and are nocturnal, venturing out only after dark. Experts in camouflage and stealth, they were thought to be invisible for many years.

While shy, the Trow is also mischievous and enjoys playing pranks on humans. They often enter peoples homes late at night to sit by the fire and make strange noises that scare anyone who is just drifting off to sleep.

Trow also love music and have been known to kidnap musicians and take them back to their dens. This is especially common with expert fiddlers.

The den of the Trow is said to be hard to enter without knowing the secret way. While their homes appear as mounds of earth from the outside, those few who have entered such a place report them to be large and lavish - often filled with gold or silver treasure.

WARNING: As with other fae creatures - should you find yourself in the den of a Trow do not take anything and NEVER eat the food. Once enchanted by fae food it is often impossible to eat anything else.

THE
BABY GOBLIN

Baby Goblins

The care and feeding of baby goblins is a strange and complex process. It varies a bit depending on the exact type of goblin, but generally their diet involves a strange combination of sour milk mixed with sweet honey. When they get older smelly cheeses, steamed spider legs, and snails may be added to their diet.

Young goblins have a long and drawn out period of teething and their baby teeth are incredibly sharp. During the first stages of teething they are given softer things to chew such as tree bark, corks, erasers, and old pencils.

As their teeth develop they switch to biting harder objects including tree roots, bottle caps, rope, and fossilized noodles.

Baby goblins have very high pitched voices and when upset their shrieks can break glass or other fragile objects so they are usually raised in a simple, sturdy environment (such as a cave or stone house) until they have outgrown throwing tantrums.

During the great wars baby goblin excrement was often weaponized due to its debilitating stench and highly flammable properties.

Goblin Fashion

Goblins have a very strange sense of fashion that has little to do with functionality. They pride themselves on bright colors, buttons, bows, and other adornments.

Goblins often gamble or trade buttons, scraps, ribbon and so forth. These bits they are constantly tacking onto their outfits which results in a very patched together and excessive look.

When a clothing item or bag needs to be secured it is usually done with a buckle or rope, buttons are decorative only and, for fashionable goblins, the more buttons the better.

A few words on Goblin Feet

Most goblins have very long, thin feet that are incredibly sensitive. The common goblin footwear consists of flexible shoes of a soft, but tough protective material (often animal hide of some sort). Due to sensitivity it is rare for goblins to expose their feet, even to each other.

These foot coverings are often decorated with stripes or other patterns. It is rare that a goblin wear full shoes unless their job requires it (such as explorers or soldiers). This is because goblin feet are very flexible and they take great pride in being able to wiggle their toes.

Goblin Hats

Goblins take great pride in their hats and consider them a symbol of prowess and superiority. As with their other garments they may be greatly patched together and embellished with various things including feathers, bird feet, sprigs of trees, ribbons, bones, buttons, and so forth.

The weight of all these fanciful additions often causes the hat to sag over the eyes and results in much stumbling about blindly. Sight, of course, is considered secondary to the quality of one's hat.

Hat Makers

The art of hat making is considered one of the most prized skills a goblin can have. Hat makers are often ranked above kings and queens in goblin hierarchy.

To become a hat maker an infant goblin is placed into a large hat and floated upon the water. If the hat sinks the goblin cannot become a hat maker, if it floats they can. When the goblin reaches eight years of age they are sent to train with an experienced hat maker.

The trainee is only allowed to make hats, talk to hats, sleep on a pile of hats, eat from a hat, and so forth for the next four years. During this time they are not allowed to wear a hat, but will be presented with an extravagant one at graduation. This results in very skilled hat makers who are also completely insane.

Goblin Hairdressing

Only the most wealthy of goblins can afford to hire a hairdresser or personal stylist. Stylist goblins are known to be very skilled with a dull blade and are usually color-blind.

Goblins value frizzy, messy, spiky hair the most and, as with their clothing, it may be adorned with a series of accessories.

Poor goblins will wear simple caps and hats to cover their hair.

Goblins with a little more money may have ribbons, bows, or other scraps of fabric tied haphazardly throughout their hair.

Those with further funds might have an assortment of road kill such as bits of dead mice or lizards knotted into their locks.

The richest of goblins will have live animals woven into their hair including worms, millipedes, small toads, and so forth. Their hairstyle requires regular care to keep it well fed and entertained.

It should be noted that in wealthy goblin circles total baldness is considered disgraceful and these goblins will either have elaborate hats or pay to have a wig made.

Common wig materials include bat, cat, and mouse fur.

THE
STYLIST

Garment Construction

Goblin garments are generally constructed by each individual goblin unless the goblin can afford a tailor. These are known as "Seam Masters" and while they are not quite as prestigious as hat makers, they are equally insane.

Seam Masters usually use tools that are very sharp, very pointy, and much too large for the task at hand. This helps create the "signature style" that goblins have (i.e. lots of jagged and uneven clothing).

Seam Masters sometimes work with personal stylists and/or hat makers if a goblin is wealthy enough to hire an entire team. They are notorious for loud, violent bickering which often results in the most wealthy of goblins wandering about completely naked.

THE SEAM MASTER

THE
DE TANGLER

TANGLER & DETANGLER

Tanglers and Detanglers are always trained in pairs. One being taught to tie knots and tangle strings while the other is taught to undo them. This tradition was started to create a well balanced workforce, but the Tangler goblins often get so annoyed at the Detangler goblins that they go nuts and kill them for untying all their tangles. The long term results are that things are generally more knotted and tangled around goblins than one would like.

PLUCKER OF BUTTONS

Acquiring Materials

Certain goblins are tasked with acquiring the materials used in goblin fashion, cooking, inventing, and so forth.

This special type of goblin is similar to an explorer but is more focused on hunting and gathering. Some goblins become obsessed with acquiring and even hoarding a specific item such as the plucker of buttons who can be held responsible for many of the puzzling missing buttons on our clothing.

One of the most famous hoarders is the self-proclaimed Queen of Feathers who went insane hunting for feathers and attempted to construct an entire kingdom out of them. Her life was tragically cut short by the great feather avalanche in June of 1843.

Goblin Explorers

Goblins that venture out into the world seeking new doodads, gadgets, creatures, and cheeses are known as Goblin Explorers.

These goblins like to be prepared for anything. REALLY. Their motto is BPAAOAATMDNO: Be Prepared for Absolutely Anything that may Occur at Any and All Times no Matter the Day, Night, or Othertime.

Goblin explorers carry the tools of their trade on their back in a series of bags and packs all tied together in a Sturdy Durty Catch-All Harness System.*

Like their motto, the pack of the goblin explorer is ridiculously excessive. A given pack will contain everything the goblin needs for hunting, camping, cooking, fishing, setting traps, picking teeth, tickling toes, swatting flies, climbing walls, digging pits, lighting fires, cutting mushrooms, falling off walls, hiding from demons, and so forth. Their pack will also contain a good number of items the goblin will never, ever, in any circumstance need no matter what should happen.

Due to the size and cumbersome nature of their packs goblin explorers move very slowly. Thus, it takes them a very, very, VERY, very, very long time to explore anything. Many packs take so long remove that explorers learn to sleep by simply leaning against a rock or tree with their pack still on.

** Patent pending by Ludwug R. Snoggswort*

Giant Beard Trimmer
Medium sized toad catcher
Sragdoodle Head Remover
Insect Impairment Implement
Ocular Shielding Devices
Slight Displacement Sticks
Dizzy makers
Fish burning pan
Food stabbing gadgets
Salty Demon Deterrent
Rope Bridge removal sheers
Magic Beans
All-In-One walking stabilizer, cauldron stirrer, and trap brace
All terrain foot coverings
Always be prepared!

Goblin Cooking

There are three "schools" to the unique art of goblin cooking:

<u>CRUNCHY:</u> This cooking style makes food as crunchy as possible. This is achieved through advanced burning and charring techniques as well as the addition of nutshells, eggshells, pebbles, and bone.

<u>SMELLY:</u> Those who practice this school of cooking focus on making food smell as bad as possible. The worse food smells the more gourmet the chef is considered. The art of achieving the most smelly food is a secret passed down from cook to cook, but rumors say it involves much stink-weed, mold, and the boiling of very old, unwashed socks.

<u>SLIPPERY:</u> Perhaps the strangest of the goblin cooking styles, Slippery Cooks focus on making food as slimy as possible. This is to aid it to "slip" down the throat as quickly as possible with no chewing required.

Cooking techniques involve coatings of slug slime and very old banana peels.

Goblin cooks of these three styles often fight and argue over which is better. Very VERY rare is the goblin who masters multiple styles. Only two goblins in history have ever mastered all three and used them together. Few can recall tasting their food as it was usually very deadly, but these master chefs are regarded with reverence and only discussed in hushed tones.

Goblin Cheese

The quality (and thus price) of a wheel of goblin cheese is directly related to how pungent it is. The most expensive of cheeses are those requiring one to pinch their nose while eating in order not to pass out.

Goblin cheese making is a long and time consuming process and there are many types of goblin cheese. These five types are the best known:

<u>PICKLED BLARG CHEESE:</u> Pickled in a vat of salt water and moldy socks, this cheese contains goat milk and bits of blarg. Blarg appears to be a meaty substance that resembles slimy liverwurst. It is unclear from what animal blarg originates, but it smells terrible.

<u>GREENROT RAT CHEESE:</u> This cheese is made from the milk of rats fed only onions and pickles. It is then wrapped in very old moss and extremely unwashed laundry and allowed to cure for many months. It is known to cause the notoriously bad breath which many goblins are very proud of.

<u>TUFTED SLIME CHEESE:</u> Starts with any cheese that is then pre-chewed by the Sragdoodle whose saliva adds a strong hint of bile. This mushy substance is pressed into molds already coated with the legs of small bugs or flies and then allowed to harden. It is known for its crusty (leg covered) shell and slimy interior textures.

<u>STINKWEED STOUT CHEESE:</u> Chopped stinkworms are allowed to mold and then mixed into a curdled milk cheese. The cheese is placed on a pike and left to air-harden for seven or eight months.

<u>SKUNK CHEESE:</u> Consists of as many other types of cheeses as a goblin can acquire, mashed and mushed together and then wrapped in moldy onion skin. This is then placed in a room with very agitated skunk for three days.

THE
FISH FETCHER

Goblin Fishing

Goblins are excellent fishermen (and women). They find the human style of fishing boring and slow. Instead they use one of two styles to catch fish.

The first is to hurl themselves headlong at a large group of fish and attempt to catch one. This is not very effective, but it is a great deal of fun and eventually results in both fish and concussions.

The second fishing style is more patient and calculated. The goblin watches quietly for a fish to swim nearby and then spears it with something sharp (which may or may not actually be a spear).

Note that goblins consider cooking fish a travesty and generally crunch them up as they are caught, scales, bones, and all.

MUSHROOM PLUCKER

Mushroom Crops

Goblins love mushrooms (though not nearly as much as they love cheese) and are known to harvest and sometimes even grow their own mushroom crops.

They are experts at identifying different types of mushrooms - easily able to tell which ones will smell the most when cooked and which are poisonous (though they often harvest those as well for certain sneaky purposes).

Goblins also hold games and contests involving mushrooms that include a form of bowling and a fungus beauty pageant.

The winner of these games is declared the mushroom king or queen, but since they occur every few days a goblin never keeps the title for very long.

Grotwarts Perfect Porridge

1 Pot Slug Slime
4 Fly Wings, dried & crushed
Glob of Sragdoodle Snot
3-6 Diced Meal Worms
1 Good Sized Dust Bunny
A pinch of powdered beetle shell

1. Bring slug slime to a simmer
2. Sprinkle in fly wings and stir in snot.
3. Add meal worms and cook until mushy.
4. Stir in dust bunny, but do NOT OVERCOOK.
5. Add Beetle shell on top and serve.

THE
PEPPERMINT PINCHER

THE
TEA MASTER

Goblin Tea

Surprisingly, goblins are great connoisseurs of tea. They drink all sorts of herbal and floral teas as well as some more unusual types of tea. Here's a sampling of a few popular goblin teas:

PEPPERMINT & HONEY: This sweet and sharp tea is the most "normal" of goblin teas and probably the only one a human could manage to ingest. It is often had with a bit of milk or cream and a side of bread and honey by very young goblins.

ONION, GARLIC & SPIT: This strong and spicy tea is used to clear just about any ailment. The type of spit used varies and can effect the flavor. Llama spit is much sought after for this tea.

ROSE PETAL & SLUG SLIME: A mild, but slippery tea that tastes of roses and the underside of a rock and tends to get stuck to the roof of your mouth.

MOLDY SOCK & LEMON GRASS: A musky, tart tea. Considered a refreshing tonic when served cold on a hot day.

POCKET LINT & NUT BRINE: A chewy and salty tea which involves the soaking of nuts in salt water and then the addition of the lint crumbled on top for texture and style.

STINK WEED & RAT DROPPING: A truly smelly tea.

SLUDGE: The soggy remnants of ten other tea brewings randomly mixed together with minimal water added.

THE NUT KING

The Nut King

The King of Nuts is a position that is not nearly so affluent as the title suggests. The crown is awarded to the goblin who is the best at opening stubborn nuts.

This goblin is then required by goblin decree to open the nuts of any goblin who should request the service. This can be time consuming and sometimes also painful.

Goblins tend to open their own nuts only behind closed, locked doors and in dark rooms. This prevents other goblins from evaluating their nut opening skills and passing the crown onto them.

For this reason the Nut King tends to hold his position for a long time, sometimes his entire adult life. Constantly opening nuts for demanding goblins at any time day or night will often wear upon the Nut King until he, himself, is nuts.

Goblin Music

Goblins are lovers of music, dance, and parties in general. Almost all goblins learn to play some form of noise maker so they can join in when a party occurs (and they frequently do, sometimes several at a time).

Instruments goblins play include: Drums, flutes, pipes, lutes, rat-gut guitars, spoons, bottles, bottle caps, scorpion tail rattles, whistles, pots n' pans, and cheese.

Goblin Juggling

Goblin Jugglers begin with simple balls and other mundane items for practice. However, for performance they are expected to use something more death defying and entertaining. This often results in goblin jugglers having very short lifespans.

Common items to juggle include man-eating plant seedlings (in pots), shards of broken glass, balls of hot wax, razor fish bones, flaming wasp stingers, and explosively moldy cheese wheels.

THE JESTER

Goblin Jesters

Jesters are employed to entertain at goblin social events including bonfires, masked balls, parties, festivals, and any other random events goblins can think up.

Goblin Jesters can be identified by their garish, clashing clothing and multi-pointed hats. These goblins are able to perform a variety of goblin entertainment which may include any of the following skills:

Joking, singing, storytelling, miming, riddling, nose whistling, really bad joke telling, ear wiggling (and flapping), walking on their hands, pyrotechnics, swallowing live bugs, stilt walking, even worse joke telling, speaking backwards, being pelted, musical burping, shadow puppetry, walking on other goblins hands, swallowing live fish, sock puppetry, really REALLY bad joking, offending other goblins, magic tricks, poorly executed illusions, slipping on fruit peels, tripping others, making poor puns, shaping snot animals, tickling man eating plants, artistic display of bodily functions, knotting of arms and/or legs, swallowing swords, and exceptionally, excessively, hideously, bad joke telling.

The Dangers of Goblin Comedy

The higher paid the jester, the more disposable he/she is for comedic purposes. This makes comedy a very high risk profession for goblins.

A goblin might take offense at a joke or one might swallow a sword the wrong way. Perhaps the fireworks get out of hand. Maybe the goblins won't be amused and will riot and trample the jester. Whatever the cause - Jesters just don't live very long. It's a profession for the thrill seekers and adrenaline junkies of the goblin world.

Goblins throwing really affluent events always hire a number of jesters so there will be a spare handy when one dies.

Thus the death of one or more jesters is considered a sign that a party is going well and is a common turn of phrase among goblins describing the event. For example one might say "You missed an amazing three jester bonfire last night!" or "The cheese social went off with a double jester!"

Recently, a market in jester insurance has started, but rather than insuring the jester's life, it instead insures that the jester will be satisfactorily funny before death. If he or she is not, the audience will be compensated.

THE OTHER
JESTER

THE FLYCATCHER

Fly Catching

Goblins catch flies both as a food source and as a casual community sport. These two things are often combined into a fly catching tournament and afternoon barbecue picnic.

Something sweet and overly ripe (moldy fruit for example) is usually used to lure flies to these events ahead of time.

Anywhere from ten to a hundred goblins might attend the event with most participating in the sport. A fly must be caught alive and at least 80% intact to be counted in the competition.

Fly catchers generally use nets, but any sort of container can be used including pots, pans, blankets, hats and so forth. There is much running, leaping and luring of the flies which creates an enjoyable acrobatic display of both goblins and flies.

The game ends when the goblins are too tired to chase further or the flies become too scarce. The goblins will then proceed to skewer the still squirming flies for seasoning and toasting over a fire pit.

Frog Riding

Frog riding is a goblin sport in which a goblin attempts to jump onto and stay on a frog's back for as many leaps as possible.

The goblin must last at least three hops of the frog to be counted as a frog rider amongst his (or her) fellow sports-goblins.

Points are awarded per leap by a panel of judges. These are based on how high and how far the frog leaps as well as how well the goblin stays on its back.

The judges are usually drunk throughout the competition and therefore not very observant or fair. This results in the riders and spectators constantly shouting at them.

If a goblin is especially displeased with a judge he will throw his sweaty, wet, socks in their face.

The current Frog Riding Champion holds a score of thirteen leaps upon the back of a very cranky bull frog.

Other goblin sports include Bug-Mitten, Stink Ball, Cockroach Wrestling, Troll Tickling, The Tossing of the Flaming Stink, and Cheese Catapulting.

THE FROGRIDER

Goblin Literacy

Many varieties of goblins can read, and even write! A good portion of the goblin community finds books to be nonsense. This may actually be true of the books written by goblins - the few volumes that have made their way into the human world make little sense.

The hardest to understand are goblin philosophy books such as the eight hundred page tome simply entitled "Meditations on Cheese" by Kelz Greenrot the Third.

More common book topics include many relating to humans such as "How NOT to get stepped on" by Thistle Drrolring and "Tormenting Larger Creatures" by Smangly Hegfoot.

While there is rarely a public library for goblins, many of the wiser goblins with extensive book collections lend them out and usually employ a Book Keeper for this purpose.

The Book Keeper is a goblin who runs about collecting books to be returned to their employer (no matter who they belonged to originally). These goblins can often be seen rushing about at great speeds with stacks of books balanced on their backs and heads. Occasional Book Keeper collisions are just another part of day to day goblin life.

THE
Book Keeper

JF '15
THE
COUNTER OF STRIPES

Goblin Mathematics

Math, for goblins, is more of an art form or game than a science. Goblins who are losing arguments are often known to proclaim "But I know MATH!" even if it has no bearing on the topic of the argument.

"Knowing math" to a goblin generally means one of the following things:

1. That they can count as high as the number of fingers and toes they have.

2. That they know someone named "Math"

The exceptions to this are goblin accountants, inventors, and counters of stripes. A Counter of Stripes is generally appointed for each goblin village or city. His or her job is to count all the stripes within their appointed domain.

Since goblins love wearing striped clothing and are constantly coming and going the count is never complete, but goblins are sure this number will one day be very important.

Goblin Time Keeping

Goblin time keeping is much more complex than human time keeping. In fact it is so complex that no one other than the Goblin Time Keepers understand it. And sometimes not even they do.

Units of time for goblins consist of Gogs, Twogs, and Squagz which all occur sometime between the sunrise of one day and the sunset of the next, but it is not clear how these units are measured or relate to one another (if they do at all). In addition some goblin pocket watches also seem to measure Sgowts and Zgauqs but their purpose is unknown.

THE
TIME KEEPER

Goblin Inventors

Goblin inventors are some of the most insane goblins and generally have no idea what they are doing. They are, however, experts in sounding like they know what they are doing and other goblins regard them as mad geniuses. In fact, the harder it is to tell what an invention actually does the better the invention is considered to be by the goblin community.

One of the most famous goblin inventions is the Twillbinder Racketing Qarling Widet. No one is sure what it does just yet, but it's very brilliant and important.

Test Subjects

Inventors need to be sure their inventions work. This requires, of course, testing them. As crazy as goblin inventors may be, they are not dumb enough to test their own (possibly fatal) inventions. For this they seek out even crazier goblins who are desperate for money, cheese, and/or excitement and hire them to be test subjects.

Testing procedures may require them to wear, ride in, or otherwise experience a given invention so the inventor can determine what adjustments or "safety" features are needed.

Testing these inventions creates a market for protective gear such as padding for the shoulders, back, stomach, elbows, and knees. It also includes a variety of eye wear in the form of stylish, if sometimes strange, goggles and safety glasses.

THE
COIN KEEPER

Goblin Economics

Goblins find the currency of humans fascinating. Many goblins collect coins and keys (it is a common goblin belief that keys are also a valuable form of payment in the human world). This is because both coins and keys are generally shiny objects and goblins are drawn to shiny things.

Goblins themselves have a very strange and ever fluctuating currency system. Whatever items are most in demand are used to measure the worth of all other items.

For example an expensive wheel of skunk cheese might be 2.3 worms and a ball of earwax.

The following week the same cheese might be valued to be worth a snail shell, 10 daisy petals, and one stubbed toe.

This confusing system means that the only consistently wealthy goblins are those sneaky enough to horde items and then start a trend that make them valuable.

Goblin Magic

Magic, for goblins, is much more chaotic, random, and explosive than for other fae creatures. Goblin Witches and Wizards often feel a calling to magic at a young age and, before long, seek an apprenticeship to learn the craft.

Goblins outside this magical community regard magic and those who practice it as scatterbrained nitwits who will probably come to a quick end.

Goblin Wizards focus mainly upon the brewing of potions that may explode or transform, but one is never sure which. Goblin Witches focus more on soothsaying and the making of magical charms.

Goblin Soldiers

Goblin Soldiers consist of the brave and mostly foolhardy goblins who choose to fight on behalf of their town, city, kingdom etc. These warriors have a confusing system of ranks that includes titles such as Troll Fodder, Canon Martyr, Pointy Brigade Leader, Sacrificial Scout, Halberd Hurler, and so forth.

The order of these ranks is not entirely clear, even to the Goblin Soldiers themselves. This leads to much arguing as each goblin feels themselves most important in a given military maneuver.

Fire Starters

All goblin armies as well as some social events make use of Fire Starters. These goblins are pyromaniacs who cannot resist lighting things on fire. This makes them handy when it comes to lighting cannons, torching enemy encampments and setting off fireworks displays. Unfortunately, they also tend to set fire to their comrades and own encampments, so they must be watched very closely at all times.

WEAPONS & ARMOR

Goblin soldiers feel that the sharper and pointier their weapons and armor, the better it is. They are determined to outdo their comrades by constantly affixing anything sharp they find to their gear.

This haphazard process does not take into account such trivial matters as visibility, flexibility, and safety.

Thus most goblin battle injuries are actually caused by the gear of the goblin himself, rather than an enemy.

SPIDER SPEAKER

Spider Speaking

A few goblins are born with the ability to converse with other animals, usually insects. Most valued of these are the Spider Speakers.

These goblins can converse with most species of spider and, given proper payment, have them perform tasks. Spiders can do useful scouting for an army, weave nets or bridges, and assist in difficult climbing tasks.

While spider speakers are useful, many other goblins avoid them finding them unnatural and creepy (much more so than wizards or witches).

Speaking to other Animals

Other animals that goblins can sometimes speak to include cats, dogs, rats, rabbits, and sometimes even squirrels.

The gift of speaking to a squirrel is both incredibly rare and revered. Young goblins are often told bedtime stories of the ancient squirrel riders, but none have been known to have this ability for the last few decades.

THE GARDEN GOBLIN

Garden Goblins

A kinder, more gentle form of goblin, Garden Goblins are part Hobgoblin or have some Brownie in their bloodlines.

These goblins are usually very helpful and will care for your plants causing flowers to bloom more often, vegetables to be larger and more flavorful, and so forth.

Garden Goblins care little for the company of other goblins and do not participate in goblin fashion at all. They are usually clad in older, more ragged clothing that has been repaired many times. Often stained with dirt, these goblins blend into the garden environment so only those who look closely can spot them.

Goblins who make a home in the garden will often act out if there are neglected plants or lots of weeds. This can result in rotten fruit and unpleasant surprises left on the doorstep.

Spending some time caring for the garden will usually calm them down. Also adding new flower beds or pots makes them happy. They particularly like roses and geraniums as well as any plants known to attract brightly colored butterflies.

Got a Goblin Problem?

Goblins can be troublesome and difficult creatures to deal with around the home. One should generally try a peaceful and humane solution first.

This begins with determining what the goblins want. You may find leaving out a bowl of milk and honey (a general faerie offering) pacifies them. Or you may need to leave a small bit of each meal out for the goblin (they love fish heads and bones).

If the goblins seem to be taking shiny things simply be sure that you don't leave any out where they can find them, save for an offering of a few coins a week. If the goblin is very greedy get a book on snares and lure it with shiny objects and cheese. Just be sure to let it go somewhere very, very, very far away from your home (another country works best).

Another way to deal with goblins is to entertain them. Books read aloud (or audio books) are a great way to keep them captivated and happy. They love fairy tales!

Creating a border of salt along windows and doors as well as wearing one's clothing inside out is also an age old deterrent against fae of all sorts.

If you find that you have truly mean goblins and need to get rid of them you should make your home as unappealing to them as possible. Keep it clean, always take the trash out, and have relaxing social gatherings (yoga groups or meditation) as often as possible.

Consider adopting a few cats or dogs - preferably those that enjoy hunting. A household full of busy, happy people and animals usually chases away mean goblins.

You may also want to hire an exterminator if the situation is drastic. This is a service commonly offered by witches, wizards, and other wise magical folk. While they may seem hard to find they have a way of making themselves known when goblin problems arise.

And remember: if all else fails... you can always move away!

CARD COLLECTOR

About the Author

Jessica Cathryn Feinberg is a driven, quirky, creative gal who resides in Tucson, Arizona with a house full of books, cats, dragons, and art supplies.

Jessica has been fascinated by goblins and other fae since she was very young and has dedicated her life to writing, drawing, painting, and following in the footsteps of mysterious creatures of all kinds.

She is best known for her dragon, clockwork, and wildlife artwork as well as her field guides to rare creatures.

You can meet Jessica at many southwest events!
For more information visit Artlair.com

www.ingramcontent.com/pod-product-compliance
Ingram Content Group UK Ltd.
Pitfield, Milton Keynes, MK11 3LW, UK
UKHW062304290726
14090UKWH00018B/879

9 781943 275205